[See page 104

"STAND OUT O' MY WAY, OR I'LL KILL YOU!"

THE
MOCCASIN RANCH

A STORY OF DAKOTA

BY
HAMLIN GARLAND
AUTHOR OF
"THE CAPTAIN OF THE GRAY-HORSE TROOP"
"MAIN-TRAVELLED ROADS" ETC.

NEW YORK AND LONDON
HARPER & BROTHERS PUBLISHERS
MCMIX

Copyright, 1909, by HAMLIN GARLAND.

All rights reserved.
Published September, 1909.

CONTENTS

CHAP.		PAGE
I.	March	1
II.	May	24
III.	June	33
IV.	August	49
V.	November	67
VI.	December	86
VII.	Conclusion	128

THE MOCCASIN RANCH

THE MOCCASIN RANCH

I

MARCH

EARLY in the gray and red dawn of a March morning in 1883, two wagons moved slowly out of Boomtown, the two-year-old "giant of the plains." As the teams drew past the last house, the strangeness of the scene appealed irresistibly to the newly arrived immigrants. The town lay behind them on the level, treeless plain like a handful of blocks pitched upon a russet robe. Its houses were mainly shanties of pine, one-story

THE MOCCASIN RANCH

in height, while here and there actual tents gleamed in the half-light with infinite suggestion of America's restless pioneers.

The wind blew fresh and chill from the west. The sun rose swiftly, and the thin scarf of morning cloud melted away, leaving an illimitable sweep of sky arching an almost equally majestic plain. There was a poignant charm in the air—a smell of freshly uncovered sod, a width and splendor in the view which exalted the movers beyond words.

The prairie was ridged here and there with ice, and the swales were full of posh and water. Geese were slowly winging their way against the wind, and ducks were sitting here and there on the ice-rimmed ponds. The sod was burned black and bare, and so firm with frost that the wagon chuckled noisily as it passed over it. The whistle of the driver

THE MOCCASIN RANCH

called afar, startling the ducks from their all-night resting-places.

One of the teams drew a load of material for a house, together with a few household utensils. The driver, a thin-faced, blue-eyed man of thirty, walked beside his horses. His eyes were full of wonder, but he walked in silence.

The second wagon was piled high with boxes and barrels of groceries and hardware, and was driven by a handsome young fellow with a large brown mustache. His name was Bailey, and he seemed to be pointing the way for his companion, whom he called Burke.

As the sun rose, a kind of transformation-scene took place. The whole level land lifted at the horizon till the teams seemed crawling forever at bottom of an enormous bowl. Mystical forms came into view—grotesquely elongated, un-

THE MOCCASIN RANCH

recognizable. Hills twenty, thirty miles away rose like apparitions, astonishingly magnified. Willows became elms, a settler's shanty rose like a shot-tower—towns hitherto unseen swam and palpitated in the yellow flood of light like shaken banners low-hung on unseen flagstaffs.

Burke marched with uplifted face. He was like one suddenly wakened in a new world, where nothing was familiar. Not a tree or shrub was in sight. Not a mark of plough or harrow—everything was wild, and to him mystical and glorious. His eyes were like those of a man who sees a world at its birth.

Hour after hour they moved across the swelling land. Hour after hour, while the yellow sun rolled up the slope, putting to flight the morning shapes on the horizon—striking the plain into level prose again, and warming the air into genial March. Hour after hour the horses toiled on till the last cabin fell away to the east, like a sail at sea, till the road faded into a trail almost imperceptible on the firm sod.

And so at last they came to the land of "the straddle-bug"—the squatters' watch dog—three boards nailed together (like a stack of army muskets) to mark a claim. Burke resembled a man taking his first sea-voyage. His eyes searched the plain restlessly, and his brain dreamed. Bailey, an old settler—of two years' experience—whistled and sang and shouted lustily to his tired beasts.

It drew toward noon. Bailey's clear voice shouted back, "When we reach that swell we'll see the Western Coteaux." The Western Coteaux! To Burke, the man from Illinois, this was

THE MOCCASIN RANCH

like discovering a new range of mountains.

"There they rise," Bailey called, a little later.

Burke looked away to the west. Low down on the horizon lay a long, blue bank, hardly more substantial than a line of cloud. "How far off are they?" he asked, in awe.

"About twenty-five miles. Our claims are just about in line with that gap." Bailey pointed with his whip. "And about twelve miles from here. We're on the unsurveyed land now."

Burke experienced a thrill of exultation as he looked around him. In the distance, other carriages were crawling like beetles. A couple of shanties, newly built on a near-by ridge, glittered like gold in the sun, and the piles of yellow lumber and the straddle-bugs increased

THE MOCCASIN RANCH

in number as they left the surveyed land and emerged into the finer tract which lay as yet unmapped. At noon they stopped and fed their animals, eating their own food on the ground beside their wagons.

While they rested, Bailey kept his eyes on their backward trail, watching for his partner, Rivers. "It's about time Jim showed up," he said, once again.

Burke seemed anxious. "They won't get off the track, will they?"

Bailey laughed at his innocence. "Jim Rivers has located about seventy-five claims out here this spring. I guess he won't lose his bearings."

"I'm afraid Blanche 'll get nervous."

"Oh, Jim will take care of her. She won't be lonesome, either. He's a great favorite with the women, always gassin'— Well, this won't feed the baby," he ended, leaping to his feet.

They were about to start on when a swift team came into sight. The carriage was a platform-spring wagon, with a man and woman in the front seat, and in the rear a couple of alert young fellows sat holding rifles in their hands and eyeing the plain for game.

"Hello!" said the driver, in a pleasant shout. "How you getting on?"

"Pretty well," replied Bailey.

"Should say you were. I didn't know but we'd fail to overhaul you."

Burke went up to the wagon. "Well, Blanche, what do you think of it—far's you've got?"

"Not very much," replied his wife, candidly. She was a handsome woman, but looked tired and a little cross, at the moment. "I guess I'll get out and ride with you," she added.

"Why, no! What for?" asked Rivers,

THE MOCCASIN RANCH

hastily. "Why not go right along out to the store with us?"

"Why, yes; that's the thing to do, Blanche. We'll be along soon," said Burke. "Stay where you are."

She sat down again, as if ashamed to give her reason for not going on with these strange men.

"I was just in the middle of a story, too," added Rivers, humorously. "Well, so long." And, cracking his whip, he started on. "We'll have supper ready when you arrive!" he shouted back.

Burke could not forget the look in his wife's eyes. She was right. It would have been pleasanter if she had stayed with him. They had been married several years, but his love for her had not grown less. Perhaps for the reason that she dominated him.

She was a fine, powerful girl, while he

THE MOCCASIN RANCH

was a plain man, slightly stooping, with thin face and prominent larynx. She had brought a little property to him, which was unusual enough to give her a sense of importance in all business transactions of the firm.

She had consented to the sale of their farm in Illinois with great reluctance, and, as Burke rode along on his load of furniture, he recalled it all very vividly, and it made him anxious to know her impression of his claim. As he took her position for a moment, he got a sudden sense of the loneliness and rawness of this new land which he had not felt before. The woman's point of view was so different from that of the adventurous man.

Twice they were forced to partly unload in order to cross ravines where the frost had fallen out, and it was growing

THE MOCCASIN RANCH

dark as they rose over the low swell, from which they could see a dim, red star, which Burke guessed to be the shanty light, even before Bailey called, exultantly:

"There she blows!"

The wind had grown chill and moist, the quacking ducks were thickening on the pools, and strange noises came from ghostly swells and hidden creeks. The tired horses moved forward with soundless feet upon the sod, which had softened during the day. They quickened their steps when they saw the lantern shine from the pole before the building.

The light of the lamp, and the sight of Blanche standing in the doorway of the cabin at the back of the store-room, was a beautiful sight to Burke. Set over against the wet, dark prairie, with its boundless sweep of unknown soil, the shanty seemed a radiant palace.

THE MOCCASIN RANCH

"Supper's all ready, Willard!" called Blanche, and the tired man's heart leaped with joy to hear the tender, familiar cadence of her voice. It was her happy voice, and when she used it men were her slaves.

Bailey came out with one of the land-seekers.

"Go in to supper, boys; we'll take care of the teams," was his hearty command.

The tired freighters gladly did as they were bid, and, scooping up some water from a near-by hollow on the sod, hurriedly washed their faces and sat down to a supper of chopped potatoes, bacon and eggs, and tea (which Blanche placed steaming hot upon the table), in such joy as only the weary worker knows.

Mrs. Burke was in high spirits. The novelty of the trip, the rude shanty, with

THE MOCCASIN RANCH

its litter of shavings, and its boxes for chairs, the bundles of hay for beds, gave her something like the same pleasure a picnic might have done. It appealed to the primeval in her. She forgot her homesickness and her vague regrets, and her smiles filled her husband with content.

Rivers and the others soon came in, and after supper there was a great deal of energetic talk. The young land-seekers were garrulous with delight over their claims, which they proudly exalted above the stumps and stones of the farms "back home."

"Why, it took three generations of my folks to clear off forty acres of land," said one of them. "They just wore themselves out on it. I told Hank he could have it, and I'd go West and see if there wasn't some land out there which wouldn't take a man's lifetime to grub out and smooth down. And I've found it."

Rivers had plainly won the friendship of Mrs. Burke, for they were having a jolly time together over by the table, where he was helping to wash the dishes. He had laughing, brown eyes, and a pleasant voice, and was one of the most popular of the lawyers and land-agents in Boomtown. There was a boyish quality in him which kept him giving and taking jocular remarks.

Bailey sometimes said: "Rivers would shine up to a seventy-year-old Sioux squaw if she was the only woman handy, but he don't mean anything by it—it's just his way. He's one o' the best-hearted fellers that ever lived." Others took a less favorable view of the land-agent, and refused to trust him.

Bailey assumed command. "Now,

fellers," he said, "we'll vamoose the ranch while Mrs. Burke turns in." He opened the way to the store-room, and the men filed out, all but Burke, who remained to put up the calico curtain with which his wife had planned to shield her bed.

Blanche was a little disturbed at the prospect of sleeping behind such a thin barrier.

"Oh, it's no worse than the sleeping-car," her husband argued.

A little later he stuck his head in at the store-room door. "All ready, Bailey."

Bailey was to sleep on the rickety lounge, which served as bedstead and chair, and the other men were to make down as best they could in the grocery.

Bailey went out to the front of the shanty to look at the lantern he had set up on a scantling. Rivers followed him.

THE MOCCASIN RANCH

"Going to leave that up there all night?"

"Yes. May keep some poor devil from wandering around all night on the prairie."

Rivers said, with an abrupt change in his voice:

"Mrs. Burke is a hummer, isn't she? How'd his flat-chested nibs manage to secure a 'queen' like that? I must get married, Bailey—no use."

Bailey took his friend's declaration more lightly than it deserved. He laughed. "Wish you would, Jim, and relieve me of the cookin'."

Blanche could hardly compose herself to sleep. "Isn't it wonderful," she whispered. "It's all so strange, like being out of the world, someway."

Burke heard the ducks quacking down in the "Moggason," and he, too, *felt* the silence and immensity of the plain out-

THE MOCCASIN RANCH

side. It was enormous, incredible in its wildness. "I believe we're going to like it out here, Blanche," he said.

Blanche Burke rose to a beautiful and busy day. The breakfast which she cooked in the early dawn was savory, and Rivers, who helped her by bringing water and building the fire, was full of life and humor. He seemed to have no other business than to "wait and tend" on her.

He called her out to see the sunrise. "Isn't this great!" he called, exultantly. Flights of geese were passing, and the noise of ducks came to them from every direction. He pointed out the distant hills, and called her attention to a solemn row of sand-hill cranes down by the swale, causing her to see the wonder and beauty of this new world.

THE MOCCASIN RANCH

"You're going to like it out here," he said, with conviction. "It is a glorious climate, and you'll soon have more neighbors than you want."

After breakfast Bailey and Burke left the "Moggason Ranch"—as Bailey called the store and shanty—to carry the lumber and furniture belonging to Burke on to his claim, two or three miles away. Rivers remained to work in the store, and to meet some other land-seekers, and Mrs. Burke agreed to stay and get dinner for them all.

During this long forenoon, Rivers exerted himself to prevent her from being lonely. He was busy about the store, but he found time to keep her fire going and to bring water and to tell her of his bachelor life with Bailey. She had never had anything like this swift and smiling service, and she felt very grateful to him.

THE MOCCASIN RANCH

He encouraged her to make some pies and to prepare a "thumping dinner." "It will seem like being married again," he said, with a chuckle.

Burke and Bailey returned at noon to dinner.

"Mrs. Burke, you can sleep in your own ranch to-night," announced Bailey.

"I guess it will be a ranch."

"It 'll be new, anyhow," her husband said, with a timid smile.

After dinner she straightened things up a little, and as she got into the wagon she said: "Well, there, Mr. Rivers. *You'll* have to take care o' things now."

Rivers leered comically, sighed, and looked at his partner. "Bailey, I didn't know what we needed before; I know now. We need a woman."

Bailey smiled. "Go get one. Don't

THE MOCCASIN RANCH

ask a clumsy old farmer like me to provide a cook."

"I'll get married to-morrow," said Rivers, with a droll inflection. They all laughed, and Burke clucked at the team. "Well, good-bye, boys; see you later."

After leaving the ranch they struck out over the prairie where no wagon-wheel but theirs had ever passed. Here were the buffalo trails, deep-worn ruts all running from northwest to southeast. Here lay the white bones of elk in shining crates, ghastly on the fire-blackened sod. Beside the shallow pools, buffalo horns, in testimony of the tragic past, lay scattered thickly. Everywhere could be seen the signs of the swarming herds of bison which once swept to and fro from north to south over the plain, all so silent and empty now.

A few antelope scurried away out of

THE MOCCASIN RANCH

the path, and a wolf sitting on a height gravely watched the teams as if marvelling at their coming. The wind swept out of the west clear and cold. The sky held no shred of cloud. The air was like some all-powerful intoxicant, and when Bailey pointed out a row of little stakes and said, "There's the railroad," their imagination supplied the trains, the wheat, the houses, the towns which were to come.

At the claim Blanche sat on a box and watched the two men as they swiftly built the little cabin which was to be her home. Their hammers rang merrily, and soon she was permitted to go inside and look up at the great sky which roofed it in. This was an emotional moment to her. As she sat there listening to the voices of the men who were drawing this fragile shelter around her, a great awe fell upon her. It seemed as if she had drawn a little nearer to the Almighty Creator of the universe. Here, where no white man had ever set foot, she was watching the founding of her own house. Was it a home? Could it ever be a home?

Swiftly the roof closed over her head, and the floor crept under her feet. The stove came in, and the flour-barrel, and the few household articles which they had brought followed, and as the sun was setting they all sat down to supper in her new home.

The smell of the fresh pine was round them. Geese were flying over. Cranes were dancing down by the ponds, prairie-chickens were *booming*. The open doorway—doorless yet—looked out on the sea-like plain glorified by the red sun just sinking over the purple line of treeless hills to the west. It was the bare, raw

THE MOCCASIN RANCH

materials of a State, and they were in at the beginning of it.

After Bailey left them the husband and wife sat in silence. When they spoke it was in low voices. It seemed as if God could hear what they said—that He was just there behind the glory of the western clouds.

II

MAY

DAY by day the plain thickened with life. Each noon a crowd of land-seekers swarmed about the Moggason Ranch asking for food and shelter, and Blanche, responding to Rivers' entreaties, went down to cook, returning each night to her bed. Rivers professed to be very grateful for her aid.

All ages and sexes came to take claims. Old men, alone and feeble, school teachers from the East, young girls from the towns of the older counties, boys not yet of age—everywhere incoming claimants

THE MOCCASIN RANCH

were setting stakes upon the green and beautiful sod.

Each day the grass grew more velvety green. Each day the sky waxed warmer. The snow disappeared from the ravines. The ice broke up on the Moggason. The ponds disappeared. Plover flew over with wailing cry. Buffalo birds, prairie pigeons, larks, blackbirds, sparrows, joined their voices to those of the cranes and geese and ducks, and the prairie piped and twittered and clacked and chuckled with life. The gophers emerged from their winter-quarters, the foxes barked on the hills, the skunk hobbled along the ravines, and the badger raised mounds of fresh soil as if to aid the boomer by showing how deep the black loam was.

Everybody was in holiday mood. Men whistled and sang and shouted and toiled —toiled terribly—and yet it did not seem

THE MOCCASIN RANCH

like toil! They sank wells and ploughed gardens and built barns and planted seeds, and yet the whole settlement continued to present the care-free manners of a great pleasure party. It seemed as if no one needed to work, and, therefore, those first months were months of gay and swift progress.

It was the most beautiful spring Blanche and Willard Burke had spent since their marriage nine years before. Blanche forgot to be petulant or moody. She was in superb health, and carried herself like a girl of eighteen. She appeared to have lost all her regrets.

She laughed heartily when Rivers came over one afternoon and boldly declared:

"Burke, I've c'me to borrow your wife. We've got a lot o' tenderfoots over there to-night, and I'm a little shy

THE MOCCASIN RANCH

of Bailey's biscuits. I'm going to carry your cook away."

"All right; only bring her back."

Blanche was a little embarrassed when Rivers replied: "I don't like to agree to do that. Mebbe you'd better come over to make sure I do."

"All right. I'll come over in time for supper." Burke's simple, good face glowed with enjoyment of the fun. He smilingly went back to beating his ploughshare with hammer and wedge as Rivers drove away with Blanche. The clink of his steel rang through the golden light that flooded the prairie, keeping time to his whistled song.

In the months of April and May the world sent a skirmish-line into this echoless land to take possession of a belt of territory six hundred miles long and one hundred miles broad. The settlers came like locusts; they sang like larks. From Alsace and Lorraine, from the North Sea, from Russia, from the Alps, they came, and their faces shone as if they had happened upon the spring-time of the world. Tyranny was behind them, the majesty of God's wilderness before them, a mystic joy within them.

Under their hands the straddle-bug multiplied. He is short-lived, this prairie insect. He usually dies in thirty days— by courtesy alone he lives. He expresses the settlers' hope and sense of justice. In these spring days of good cheer he lived at times to sixty days—but only on stony ground or fire-scarred, peaty lowlands.

He withered—this strange, three-legged, voiceless insect—but in his stead arose a beetle. This beetle sheltered human beings, and was called a shack.

THE MOCCASIN RANCH

They were all alike, these shacks. They had roofs of one slant. They were built of rough lumber, and roofed with tarred paper, which made all food taste of tar.

They were dens but little higher than a man's head, and yet they sheltered the most joyous people that ever set foot to earth. In one cabin lived a girl and a canary-bird, all alone. In the next a man who cooked his own food when he did not share his rations with the girl, all in frank and honorable companionship. On the next claim were two schoolteachers, busy as magpies, using the saw and hammer with deft accuracy. In the next was a bank-clerk out for his health—and these clean and self-contained people lived in free intercourse without slander and without fear. Only the Alsatians settled in groups, alien and unapproachable. All others met at odd

THE MOCCASIN RANCH

times and places, breathing in the promiseful air of the clean sod, resolute to put the world of hopeless failure behind them.

Spring merged magnificently into summer. The grass upthrust. The waterfowl passed on to the northern lake-region. The morning symphony of the prairie-chickens died out, but the whistle of the larks, the chatter of the sparrows, and the wailing cry of the nesting plover came to take its place.

The gophers whistled and trilled, the foxes barked from the hills, and an occasional startled antelope or curious wolf passed through the line of settlement as if to see what lay behind this strange phalanx of ploughmen guarding their yellow shanties.

Week after week passed away, and the government surveyors did not appear. The Boomtown *Spike* told in each issue

THE MOCCASIN RANCH

how the men of the chain and compass were pushing westward; but still they did not come, and the settlers' hopes of getting their claims filed before winter grew fainter. The mass of them had planned to take claims in the spring, live on them the required six months, "prove up," and return East for the winter.

In spite of these disappointments, all continued to be merry. No one took any part of it very seriously. The young men went out and ploughed when they pleased, and came in and sat on the door-step and talked with the women when they were weary. The shanties were hot and crowded, but no one minded that; by-and-by they were to build bigger.

And, then, all was so new and beautiful, and the sky was so clear. Oh, that marvellous, lofty sky with just clouds enough to make the blue more intense! Oh, the

THE MOCCASIN RANCH

wonder of the wind from the wild, mysterious green sea to the west! With the change and sheen of the prairie, incessant and magical life was made marvellous and the winter put far away.

Merry parties drove here and there visiting. Formalities counted for little, and yet with all this freedom of intercourse, this close companionship, no one pointed the finger of gossip toward any woman. The girls in their one-room huts received calls from their bachelor neighbors with the confidence that comes from purity of purpose, both felt and understood. Life was strangely idyllic during these spring days. Envy and hate and suspicion seemed exorcised from the world.

III

JUNE

THE centre of the social life was Bailey's store. There stood the post-office, which connected the settlers with the world they had left behind. There they assembled each day when the flag ran up the long pole which stood before the door as a signal for the mail. On the treeless, shrubless prairie one could see the flag miles away, as it rose like a faint fleck of pink against the green of the prairie beyond or the blue sky above.

Twice a week Rivers drove out with

supplies. These were the eventful days of the week, and it was significant to observe with what tasteful care the young women thought it proper to dress on this day. Hats, dainty and fresh, cool muslins, spotless cuffs, ribbons. They came out of their cabins with all the little airs and graces of their Eastern homes. Bailey shared their good opinion, but he was always silent and a little timid in their presence, and usually disappeared as soon as Rivers came. "The social responsibilities belong to you, partner," he was accustomed to say.

As the summer wore on, the number of those pathetically eager for letters increased. The sun-bright plain, the beautiful, almost cloudless sky, and the ever-flooding light wore upon them. They began to recall wistfully the cool streams of New England, the wooded slopes of

THE MOCCASIN RANCH

Wisconsin, the comfortable homesteads and meadows of Illinois, and they came for their mail with shining eyes—and when forced to say "Nothing to-day," Bailey always suffered a keen pang of sympathetic pain.

He himself watched the eastern horizon, incessantly and unconsciously, hours before the wagon was due, and, when it came in sight at last, ran his flag up along its mast joyously.

It was a great pleasure to him to sit and talk with his partner, and he looked forward to his visits eagerly. To Jim he could utter himself freely. They had known each other so long, and he believed he understood his partner to the centre of his heart.

He usually had supper ready—often he had help from the girls or Mrs. Burke, and while a dozen hands volunteered at

THE MOCCASIN RANCH

the team and with the mail-bag, Rivers was free to hurry to his table, whereat he fared like a pasha attended by the flower of his harem. The girls pretended it was all on account of his office as mail-carrier, but they deceived no one, much less an experienced beau like Rivers. He accepted it all with shameless egotism.

To Bailey's mind Jim was too well attended. He seemed to see less and less of his partner as the season wore on. They seldom sat down to talk in the good old fashion, wearing out half the night smoking, listening to the slumber-song of the night plain, for Rivers got into the habit of walking home with some of the girls after the mail was distributed, leaving his partner to do the trading. Sometimes he went away with Mrs. Burke, if she were alone; sometimes with Estelle Clayton, whom Bailey thought the finest woman in the world. He secretly resented Rivers' attention to Estelle, for he had come to look upon her as under his protection. Her coming raised mail-days to the level of a national holiday.

She scared him, and yet he rejoiced to see her coming down over the sod so strong, so erect, so clear-eyed. She wore her hair like a matron, and that pleased him, and she looked at him so frankly and unwaveringly. She had been a school-teacher in some middle Western State, and had been swept into this movement by her desire to go to an Eastern college.

Bailey contrived to look very stern and very busy whenever she came in, but she was wise in ways of men, and treated him as if he were a good comrade, and so gradually he came to talk to her almost as freely as with Blanche Burke.

He did not know that Jim almost invariably went over to Burke's shanty—even when he walked home with Miss Clayton. Rivers did not impress Estelle favorably. She was not one to be moved by flattery, nor by dimples in male cheeks. She accepted his company pleasantly, but there were well-defined bounds to her friendship, as Rivers discovered one evening as they were walking over the plain toward her home.

On every side the vivid green stretched away, smooth as the rounded flesh of a woman, velvet in texture, glorified by the saffron and orange of the sunset sky.

At the cabin they met Carrie, for whom Estelle was both sister and mother. The little shanty slanted on the side of a swell like a little boat sliding up a mon-

THE MOCCASIN RANCH

strous mid-ocean wave. Around it lay a little garden inhabited by a colony of chicken-coops—"All my own making," Estelle said. "Oh, of course, sister held the nails and bossed, but I did it. I like it, too. It's more fun than working red poppies on tidies—that's about all they'll let you do back East."

"It doesn't matter much what you do out here," said Rivers, meaningly.

"Oh yes, it does. Some things are wrong anywhere; but there are other things which people *think* are wrong that are only unusual," she answered, and he knew she knew what he meant.

The talk moved on to lighter themes, and then died away as the three sat in the doorway and saw the light fade out of the sky.

Carrie's thin, eager face shone with angelic light. She seemed to hold her

THE MOCCASIN RANCH

breath as flame after flame of the marvellous light was withdrawn.

"Oh, the sky is so big out here," she whispered. Estelle locked hands with her and sat in silence. Rivers, awkward and constrained, respected their emotion. At last he rose.

"I'm going over to Burke's a little while, so I'll have to be moving."

"Mrs. Burke is very strange," said Estelle; "I can't seem to get on with her. She seems very lonely and restless. Her husband is away a great deal, but I can't get her to talk, when I call, and she never returns my call."

"She never seemed that way to me," Rivers said, having nothing better in mind at the moment.

"I think she's homesick. I wish I knew how to help her, but I don't."

Rivers walked away with two thoughts

THE MOCCASIN RANCH

in his mind. One was the girl's sentence about things that were wrong and things which people thought were wrong, and the other was the question about Blanche—was she homesick? That puzzled him. Had he only seen her in her joyous moods? It was not pleasant to think of her growing sad—perhaps on his account.

Burke sat on a bench outside the door, smoking silently in the dusk. Blanche was stirring about inside.

"Hello, Rivers!" Burke called. "Take a seat." He pointed at a vinegar-keg.

Blanche hurried to meet her visitor, a beautiful smile on her face. "Come inside," she said. "I've got some work to do, and I want to hear you men talk." They obediently complied, and she lighted a lamp. "I like to see you when you talk," she added, flashing a smile at Rivers.

He saw the change in her for the first time. She certainly was paler, her face less boyish, and a deeper shadow hovered about her eyes.

"I came over to see if you wouldn't come down and help us get up a jollification at the store on the Fourth," he said.

"Why, of course. What shall I do?"

"Oh, stir up a cake—and make some ice-cream. Can you make ice-cream?"

"You bet I can—with ice. Bring on your ice."

"Ice is easy to get. Cook is what bothered me."

"That ought to be easy," said Burke. "Marry one."

"That's what I'm telling Bailey."

"Why don't you set the example. 'Stelle Clayton—now."

Rivers laughed, but his eyes, directed

above Burke's head, met the unsmiling gaze of Blanche and sobered.

"Miss Clayton and I don't seem to get along first-rate," he said, and her face lighted again.

"Well, there are lots of others 'round here—lonesome girls. Blanche, can't you help Jim find a woman?"

Blanche did not answer lightly. She turned to her work. "I guess he can find one if he tries hard."

She was alluring as she kneaded the bread at the table. The flex of her waist and the swing of her skirts affected Rivers powerfully. He watched her in silence. Once she looked around, and the penetrative glance of his eyes filled her face with a rush of blood, and her eyes misted. A few minutes later he said "good-night" in an absent-minded way and went home.

Burke talked on, attempting to retain the cheery atmosphere which Rivers had brought in, but Blanche refused to answer, a sombre look on her sullen face. She seemed falling back into her old petulant, moody ways, and her husband suffered a corresponding dejection.

The elation was passing out of his heart. Their picnic was at an end.

As the summer came on he was forced to go out ploughing for other settlers, and she was left alone a great deal. This was hard to bear. There was so little to do in her little sun-smit cabin, and her trip to the post-office to get the mail and to meet the other settlers came to be a necessity. Like the other women, she put on her best hat and gown when she went to the store, and a low word of compliment from Rivers, as he handed out the mail, put a color into her face and a joy in her heart which her husband had never been able to arouse—indeed, it was after these visits that she was most cruel to Willard.

Sometimes she went with him to visit the neighbors, but not often. One day he said:

"I'm goin' to work f'r Jim Bradley to-day—want 'o go 'long?"

"I can't this mornin'. Perhaps I'll come over after dinner and walk home with you."

"I think you'll like Mrs. Bradley. She's got the purtiest little baby you ever saw." He did not look at her as he slung his pick and shovel on his shoulder. "Well, I'll tell her you'll be over about three o'clock."

"All right, tell her. Mebbe I'll come and mebbe I won't," she answered, ungraciously.

THE MOCCASIN RANCH

All that forenoon she went about her little cabin moodily, or sat silently by the open door watching the buffalo birds or larks as they came up about the barn for food. The green plain was all a-shimmer with pleasant heat. The plover, nesting in the grass, were nearly ready to bring forth their young—and the mother fox had already begun to lead her litter out upon the sunny hillside; only this childless woman seemed unhappy—sad.

As she came to the cabin of the Bradleys, Willard, sunk to his topknot in the ground, was burrowing like a badger in the clay, quite oblivious to the world above him. Some one was singing in the cabin, and, approaching the door, Blanche saw a picture which thrilled her with a strange, hungry, envious passion.

A young woman was seated in the tiny

room with her back to the door, her hand on a cradle, and as she rocked she sang softly. She was a plain little woman, the cradle was cheap and common, and her singing was only a monotonous chant; but the scene had a sort of sublimity— it was so old, so typical, and so beautiful.

The woman without the threshold stood for a long time staring straight before her, then turned and walked away homeward—past the weary, patient, heroic man toiling deep in the earth for her sake—leaving him without a glance or a word.

"You didn't get over to Mrs. Bradley's this afternoon, then?" Burke said, at supper.

"No," she replied, shortly, "I had some sewin' to do."

"Wal, go to-morrow. That's an awfully cute little chap—that baby," he went on, after a little. "Mrs. Bradley let him set on my knee to-day." Then he sighed. "I wisht we had one like 'im, Blanche." After a pause, he said, "Mebbe God will send one some day."

She didn't appear to hear, and her face was dark with passion.

IV

AUGUST

NOW the settlers began to long for rain. Day after day vast clouds rose above the horizon, swift and portentous, domed like aerial mountains, only to pass with a swoop like the flight of silent, great eagles, followed by a trailing garment of dust. Often they lifted in the west with fine promise, only to go muttering and bellowing by to the north or south, leaving the sky and plain as beautiful, as placid, and as dry as before. The people grew anxious, and some of them became bitter, but the most of them kept up good courage, feeling certain that this was an unusual season.

One sultry day, while Rivers was on his way out to the store, he fell to studying the sky and air. On the prairie, as on the sea, one studies little else. There was something formidable in every sign. In the west a prodigious dome of blue-black cloud was rising, ragged at the edge, but dense and compact at the horizon.

"That means business," Rivers said to himself, and chirped to his team.

The air was close and hot. The southern wind had died away. There was scarcely a sound in all the landscape save the regular clucking of the wagon-wheels, the soft, rhythmical tread of the horses' feet, and the snapping buzz of the grasshoppers rising from the weeds. Far away to the west lay the blue Coteaux,

THE MOCCASIN RANCH

thirty miles distant, long, low, without break, like a wall. The sun was hidden by the cloud, and as he passed a shanty Rivers saw the family eating their supper outside the door to escape the smothering heat.

He smiled as he saw the gleam of white dresses about the door of the store. As he drove up, a swarm of impatient folk came out to meet him. The girls waved their handkerchiefs at him, and the men raised a shout.

"You're late, old man."

"I know it, but that makes me all the more welcome." He heaved the mail-bag to Bailey. "There's a letter for every girl in the crowd, I know, for I wrote 'em."

"We'll believe that when we see the letters," the girls replied.

He dismounted heavily. "Somebody

put my team up. I'm hungry as a wolf and dry as a biscuit."

"The poor thing," said one of the girls. "He means a cracker."

Estelle Clayton came out of the store. "Supper's all ready for you, Mr. Mail-Carrier. Come right in and sit down."

"I'm a-coming—now watch me," he replied, with intent to be funny.

The girls accompanied him into the little living-room.

"Oh, my, don't some folks live genteel? See the canned peaches!"

"And the canned lobster!"

"And the hot biscuit!"

"Sit down, Jim, and we'll pour the tea and dip out the peaches."

Rivers seated himself at the little pine table. "I guess you'd better whistle while you're dipping the peaches," he said, pointedly.

Miss Thompson dropped the spoon. "What impudence!"

"Oh, let him go on—don't mind him," said Estelle. "Let's desert him; I guess that will make him sorry."

Upon the word they all withdrew, and Rivers smiled. "Good riddance," said he.

Miss Baker presently opened the door, and, shaking a letter, said, "Don't you wish you knew?"

He pretended to hurl a biscuit at her, and she shut the door with a shriek of laughter.

Mrs. Burke slipped in. Her voice was low and timid, her face sombre.

"I cooked the supper, Jim."

"You did? Well, it's good. The biscuits are delicious." He looked at her as only a husband should look—intimate, unwaveringly, secure. "You're looking fine!"

THE MOCCASIN RANCH

She flushed with pleasure. As she passed him with the tea, he put his arm about her waist.

"Be careful, Jim," she said, gently, and with a revealing, familiar, sad cadence in her voice.

He smiled at her boyishly. He was beautiful to her in this mood. "I was hoping you'd come over and stew something up for me. Hello, there's the thunder! It's going to rain!"

Another sudden boom, like a cannon-shot, silenced the noise inside for an instant, and then a sudden movement took place, the movement of feet passing hurriedly about, and at last only one or two persons could be heard. When Rivers re-entered the store Bailey was alone, standing in the door, intently watching the coming storm. It was growing dusk on the plain, and the lightning was beginning to play rapidly, low down toward the horizon.

"We're in for it!" Bailey remarked, very quietly. "Cyclone!"

"Think so?" said Rivers, carelessly.

"Sure of it, Jim. That cloud's too wide in the wings to miss us this time."

A peculiar, branching flash of lightning lay along the sky, like a vast elm-tree, followed by a crashing roar.

Blanche cried out in alarm.

"Now, don't be scared. It's only a shower and will soon be over," said Bailey. "Here's a letter for you."

She took the letter and read it hastily, looking often at the coming storm. She seemed pale and distraught.

"Do you s'pose I've got time to get home now?" she asked, as she finished reading.

"No," said Rivers, so decidedly that Bailey looked up in surprise.

"Can't you take me home?"

Rivers looked out of the door. "By the time we get this wagon unloaded and the team hitched up, the storm will be upon us. No. I guess you're safest right here."

There was a peculiar tone, a note of authority, in his voice which puzzled Bailey quite as much as her submission.

They worked silently and swiftly, getting the barrels of pork and oil and flour into the store, and by the time they had emptied the wagon the room was dark, so dark that the white face of the awed woman could be seen only as a blotch of gray against the shadow.

They lighted the oil lamps, which hung in brackets on the wall, and then Rivers said to Blanche: "Won't you go into the other room? We must stay here and look after the goods."

"No, no! I'd rather be here with you; it's going to be terrible."

"Hark!" said Bailey, with lifted hands; "there she comes!"

Far away was heard a continuous, steady, low-keyed, advancing hum, like the rushing of wild horses, their hoof-beats lost in one mighty, throbbing, tumultuous roar; then a deeper darkness fell upon the scene, and swift as the swoop of an eagle the tornado was upon them.

The advancing wall of rain struck the building with terrific force. The lightning broke forth, savage as the roar of siege-guns. The noise of the wind and thunder was deafening. The plain grew black as night, save when the lightning flamed in countless streams across the clouds. The cabin shook like a frightened hound. Bailey looked around.

"We must move the goods!" he shouted above the tumult. "See, the rain is beating in!"

Rivers, with Blanche encircled by his arm, pressed her to his side reassuringly. "Don't be afraid. It can't blow down," he repeated.

He then leaped to Bailey's assistance, and, while the thunder crashed in their ears and the lightning blinded their eyes, they worked like frantic insects to move the goods away from the western wall, through which the rain was beating. There was a pleasure in this assault which the woman could not share. It was battle, absorbing and exalting. Their shouts were full of joyous excitement.

Once, when the structure trembled and groaned with the shock of a frightful

THE MOCCASIN RANCH

blast, Rivers again put his arm around Blanche, saying: "It can't blow over. See those heavy barrels? If this store blows down, there won't be a shanty standing in the county."

She pushed to the window to get a glimpse of the sod when the lightning flamed. She imagined the plain as it would look with every cabin flattened to earth, its inmates scattered, unhoused in the scant, water-weighted grass.

As they all stood staring out, Rivers pointed and shouted to Bailey, "See that flag-pole!"

It was made of hard pine, tough and supple, but it bent in the force of the wind like a willow twig. Again and again it bowed, rose with a fling, only to be borne down again. At last it broke with a crash; the upper half, whirling down, struck the roof, opening a ragged hole through which the rain streamed in torrents.

Rivers cried, in battle alarm, "The roof is going!"

"No, it ain't!" trumpeted Bailey, sturdily; "swing a tub up here to catch the water!"

The woman forgot her fears and aided the two men as they toiled to cover the more perishable goods with bolts of cotton cloth, while the appalling wind tore at the eaves and lashed the roof with broadsides of rain and hail, which fell in constantly increasing force, raising the roar of the storm in key, till it crackled viciously. The tempest had the voice of a ravenous beast, cheated and angry. Outside the water lay in sheets. The whole land was a river, and the shanty was like a boat beached on a bar in the swash of it.

THE MOCCASIN RANCH

Nothing more could be done, and so they waited, Bailey watching at the window, Blanche and Rivers standing in the centre of the room. Bailey came back once to say: "This beats anything I ever saw. There will be ruin to many a shanty out of this," he added, as the roar began to diminish. "Nothing saved us but our ballast of pork and oil."

"As soon as it stops, Bob, I wish you'd hitch up for me. I want to take Mrs. Burke home."

"All right, Jim; it's letting up now. I wonder if the storm was as bad over where the Clayton girls are?" His voice betrayed anxiety greater than he knew. Rivers looked at him indulgently and smiled at Blanche. "You'd better go and see," he said.

As soon as it became possible to carry a light, Bailey went to the barn and brought the team to the door. Rivers helped Blanche to a seat in the wagon and drove off across the plain, leaving Bailey alone in the water-soaked storeroom. After a half-hour's work he, too, set out on a tour of exploration. The moon was shining on the plain as serenely as if only a dew had fallen. Water stood in shallow basins here and there, but the land was unmarked of the passion of lightning and of wind. Bailey walked across the level waste, straining his eyes ahead to see if the homes of his neighbors were still standing. He saw lights gleaming here and there like warning lamps of distant schooners, and when the infrequent, silent lightning flamed over the level waste, he caught glimpses of familiar shanties standing on the low swells.

He hurried forward, his feet splashing

THE MOCCASIN RANCH

in water, too intent to turn aside. Wherever a lamp burned steadily he knew a roof still remained, and his heart grew lighter. He came at last to the object of his search. It was only a small hut, but it was to him most sacred. He knocked timidly at the door.

"Who's there?" was the quick and startled reply.

"It's Bailey. I'm here to see how you came through the storm."

"Oh, Mr. Bailey!" replied Estelle. She opened the door. "Come in. We're all right, but wet. Don't step in the pans."

As he entered, with eyes a little dazzled by the candle, Carrie, wrapped in a shawl, rose from the bed. "Oh, I'm glad to see a man! Wasn't it terrible?" Pans were set about the room to catch the dripping water. The little shanty, usually so orderly and cheerful, looked dishevelled and desolate.

Estelle laughed and said, "I tried to save the chickens, and I nearly blew away myself."

Her cheeks were flushed, and her wet hair streamed down her back. She was barefooted, a fact which she tried to conceal by leaning forward a little.

"It was very good of you to come over," she went on, more soberly, in the pause which followed. "We were scared; no use denying that, but we were too busy to dwell upon it. The wind took the tarred paper off the roof and let the rain through everywhere. It was the most exciting experience of our lives."

She was more breathless and girlish than she had ever been in his presence, and he grew correspondingly secure. A subtle charm came from her streaming

THE MOCCASIN RANCH

hair and her uncorseted and graceful figure. He offered assistance, but she sturdily replied:

"Oh no, thank you. There's nothing to do till morning, anyway. We kept the bed dry, and so we can sleep." She smiled on him with something happy hidden in the tones of her voice. She was embarrassed, but not afraid. She trusted him perfectly, and he was exalted by that trust.

"Well, I'll be over in the morning and see how badly damaged you are. I couldn't go to bed till I knew you were all right."

"Thank you. You're very kind."

He went out with a feeling that Carrie was trying hard not to laugh at him. He was sure he heard a smothered giggle as he went down the slope. He glowed with admiration for Estelle, so frank, so womanly. They seemed to have drawn closer to each other in that fifteen minutes' talk than in all the preceding months. In the joy of this deepening friendship he splashed contentedly back to the store, unheeding the pools beneath his feet.

V

NOVEMBER

SEPTEMBER and October passed before the surveyors, long looked for, came through, and three months dragged out their slow length before the pre-emptors could file and escape from their claims.

By the first of November the wonder had gone out of the life of the settlers. One by one the novelties and beauties of the plain had passed away or grown familiar. The plover and blackbird fell silent. The prairie-chicken's piping cry ceased as the flocks grew toward ma-

THE MOCCASIN RANCH

turity, and the lark and cricket alone possessed the russet plain, which seemed to snap and crackle in the midnight frost, and to wither away in the bright midday sun.

Many of the squatters by this time had spent their last dollar, and there was little work for them to do. Each man, like his neighbor, was waiting to "prove up." They had all lived on canned beans and crackers since March, and they now faced three months more of this fare. Some of them had no fuel, and winter was rapidly approaching.

The vast, treeless level, so alluring in May and June, had become an oppressive weight to those most sensitive to the weather, and as the air grew chill and the skies overcast, the women turned with apprehensive faces to the untracked northwest, out of which the winds swept pitilessly cold and keen. The land of the straddle-bug was gray and sad.

One day a cold rain mixed with sleet came on, and when the sun set, partly clear, the Coteaux to the west rose like a marble wall, crenelated and shadowed in violet, radiant as the bulwarks of some celestial city; but it made the thoughtful husband look keenly at the thin walls of his cabin and wonder where his fuel was to come from. In this unsheltered land, where coal was high and doctors far away, winter was a dreaded enemy.

The depopulation of the newly claimed land began. Some of the girls went back never to return; others settled in Boomtown, with intent to visit their claims once a month through the winter; but a few, like the Burkes, remained in their little shanties, which looked still more like dens when sodded to the eaves. The

THE MOCCASIN RANCH

Clayton girls flitted away to Wheatland, leaving the plain desolately lonely to Bailey. One by one the huts grew smokeless and silent, until at last the only English-speaking woman within three miles was old Mrs. Bussy, who swore and smoked a pipe, and talked like a man with bronchitis. She was not an attractive personality, and Mrs. Burke derived little comfort from her presence.

Willard was away a great deal teaming, working desperately to get something laid up for the winter. The summer excursion, with its laughter, its careless irresponsibility, had become a deadly grapple with the implacable forces of winter. The land of the straddle-bug had become a menacing desert, hard as iron, pitiless as ice.

Now the wind had dominion over the lonely women, wearing out their souls

THE MOCCASIN RANCH

with its melancholy moanings and its vast and wordless sighs. Its voices seemed to enter Blanche Burke's soul, filling it with hunger never felt before. Day after day it moaned in her ears and wailed about the little cabin, rousing within her formless desires and bitter despairs. Obscure emotions, unused powers of reason and recollection came to her. She developed swiftly in sombre womanhood.

Sometimes Mrs. Bussy came across the prairie, sometimes a load of land-seekers asked for dinner, but mainly she was alone all the long, long days. She spent hours by the window watching, waiting, gazing at the moveless sod, listening to the wind-voices, companioned only by her memories. She began to perceive that their emigration had been a bitter mistake, but her husband had not yet acknowledged it, and she honestly tried not to reproach him for it. Nevertheless, she had moments of bitterness when she raged fiercely against him.

Little things gave her opportunity. He came home late one day. She greeted him sullenly. He began to apologize:

"I didn't intend to stay to supper, but Mrs. Bradley—"

"Mrs. Bradley! Yes, you can go and have a good time with Mrs. Bradley, and leave me here all alone to rot. It'd serve you right if I left you to enjoy this fine home alone."

He trembled with agony and weakness.

"Oh, you don't mean that, Blanche—"

"For Heaven's sake, don't call me pet names. I'm not a child. If I'd had any sense I'd never have come out here. There's nothing left for us but just freeze or starve. What did we ever leave Illinois for, anyway?"

He sank back into a corner in gentle, sorrowful patience, waiting for her anger to wear itself out.

While they sat there in silence they heard the sound of hoofs on the frozen ground, and a moment later Bailey's pleasant voice arose: "Hullo, the house!" Burke went to the door, and Blanche rose to meet the visitor with a smile, the knot in her forehead smoothed out. There was no alloy in her pure respect and friendship for Bailey.

He came in cheerily, his hearty voice ringing with health and good-will. He took her hand in his with a quick, strong grip, and the light of his brown eyes brought a glow to her heart.

"I've come over to see if you don't want to go to the city to-morrow? I've got Joe Pease to stay in the store, and so I thought I'd take an outing."

Burke looked at his wife; she replied, eagerly:

"I should like to go, Mr. Bailey, very much. Our old team is so feeble we daren't drive so far. I'm afraid every time old Dick stumbles he'll fall down on the road."

"We'll have to get back to-morrow night," Burke said.

"Oh, we'll do that all right," replied Bailey.

As she planned the trip with tremulous eagerness, Bailey studied her. She was paler than he had ever seen her, and more refined and thoughtful, scarcely recognizable as the high-colored, powerful woman for whom he had helped build the shanty in March. There were times now when it seemed as if she were appealing to him, and his heart ached with undefined sorrow as he looked about her prison-like home.

For half an hour she chatted with something of her old-time vivacity, but when he went out her face resumed its gloomy lines, and she silenced her husband with a glance when he attempted to keep up the cheerful conversation.

The next morning, as she was dressing, she turned sick and faint for a moment. Her breath seemed to fail her, and she sat down, dizzy and weak. She was alone, but the red blood came swelling back into her face as she waited.

She grew better soon, and rose and went about her work. Then the excitement and pleasure of her trip, the expectation of meeting Rivers, helped her to put her weakness away.

Bailey called for the Clayton girls, who were making their monthly visit to their claim, and Mrs. Burke, seeing the shine of a lover's joy in Bailey's face, and the clear, unwavering trust of a pure, good girl in Estelle's gray eyes, fell silent, and the shadow of her own sorrow came back upon her face.

The ride seemed short, and the town at the end wondrously exciting. Rivers met them at the hotel, and insisted on their being his guests during their stay. They had a jolly supper together, after which they all went to the little town-hall to see a play. Blanche sat beside Rivers, and as she laughed at Si Peasley and his misadventures in the city she was girlishly happy. It was not very much of an entertainment, but in contrast with life in a sod shanty it was all very exciting for her.

THE MOCCASIN RANCH

"Oh, I wish we could live in town this winter!" she sighed in Rivers' ear.

"You can," he answered, with significant inflection.

Altogether, the evening was one of deep pleasure for Blanche. She enjoyed the companionship of the Clayton girls, who had never been so friendly and sympathetic with her before. They invited her to spend the night with them, which pleased her very much, and they all sat up till one o'clock, talking upon all sorts of tremendously interesting feminine subjects.

Next morning Estelle went with her while she did a little shopping—pitifully little, for she only had a dollar or two to spend—while Bailey loaded up his team. At last, and all too soon, her outing ended, and she faced the west with heavy heart.

THE MOCCASIN RANCH

Poor Willard also felt the menace of the desolate, wild prairie, but he had no conception of the tumult of regret and despair which filled his wife's mind as she climbed into the wagon for their return journey. She was like a prisoner whose parole had ended.

The Clayton girls said good-bye with pity in their voices, and Rivers sought opportunity to say, privately: "I hate to see you back out there on the border. If you need anything, let me know."

"All aboard!" called Bailey, as he took his reins in hand.

A bitter blast and a gray sky confronted them as they drove out of the town, and not even Bailey's abounding vitality and good-humor could keep Blanche from sinking back into gloomy silence. The wind was keen, strong, prophetic of the snows which were already gathering far

THE MOCCASIN RANCH

in the north, and the journey seemed endless; and when late in the afternoon they drew up before the squat, low hovel in which she was to spend a long and desolate winter, Blanche was shivering violently, and so depressed that she could not coherently thank the kindly young fellow who had afforded her this brief respite from her care. She staggered into the house, so stiff she could scarcely walk, and sank into a chair to sob out her loneliness and despair, while Willard pottered about building a fire on their icy hearth.

Willard Burke had a question to ask, and that night, as they were sitting at their poor little table, he plucked up courage to begin:

"Blanche, I want to ask you something—that is, I've been kind o' noticin' you—" Here he paused, intending to be sly and suggestive. "Seems to me this climate ain't so bad, after all; you complain a good deal, but seems to me you hadn't ought to." He trembled while he smiled. "It's done a lot for you."

"What do you mean?" she asked, her face flushing with confusion.

"I mean"—he tried to laugh—"your best dress seems pretty tight for you. Oh, if it only should be—"

"Don't be a fool," she angrily replied. "If anything like that happens, I'll let you know."

His face lengthened, and the smile went out of his eyes. He accepted her tone as final, too loyal to doubt her word. "Don't be mad; I was only in hopes." He rose after a silence and went out with downcast head.

She sat rigidly, feeling as if the blood

THE MOCCASIN RANCH

were freezing in her hands and feet. The crisis was upon her. The time of her judgment was coming—and she was alone! She burned with anger against Rivers. Why had he waited and waited? "*He* can put things off—he is a man, but I am the woman—I must suffer it all." The pain, the shame, the deadly danger—all were hers.

Burke returned, noisily, stamping his feet like a boy.

"It's snowin' like all git out," he said, "and I've got to rig up some kind of a sled. I reckon winter has come in earnest now, and our coal-pile is low."

He went to sleep with the readiness of a child, and as she lay listening to his quiet breath she remembered how easy it had once been for her to sleep. She had the same agony of pity for him that she would have felt for a child she had wronged malevolently.

The next day Mrs. Bussy came over. At her rap Blanche called, "Come in," but remained seated by the fire.

The old woman entered, knocking the snow off her feet like a man.

"How de do, neighbor?"

Blanche drew her shawl a little closer around her. "Not very well; sit down, won't you?"

"Can't stop. You don't seem very peart. I want to know what seems to be the trouble." Her keen eyes had never seemed so penetrating before. Blanche flushed and moved uneasily. She was afraid of the old creature, who seemed half-man, half-woman.

"Oh, I don't know. Rheumatism, I guess."

"That so? Well, this weather is

'nough to give anybody rheumatiz. I tell Ed—that's my boy—I tell Ed we made holy fools of ourselves comin' out here. I never see such a damn country f'r wind." She rambled on about the weather for some time, and at last rose. "Well, I wanted to borrow your wash-boiler; mine leaks like an infernal old sieve, and I dasen't go to town to get it mended for fear of a blow. What's trouble?"

Blanche suddenly put her hand to her side and grew white and rigid. Then the blood flamed into her cheeks, and the perspiration stood out on her forehead. She clinched her lips between her teeth and lay back in her chair.

"Ye look kind o' faint. Can't I do something for ye? Got any pain-killer? That's good, well rubbed in," volunteered the old woman.

"No, no, I—I'm all right now, it was

just a sharp twinge, that's all—you'll find the boiler in the shed; I don't need it." Her tone was one of dismissal.

The old woman rose. "All right, I'll find it. Set still." As she went out she grinned—a mocking, sly, aggravating grin. "It's all right—nothin' to be ashamed of. I've had ten. I called *my* first one pleurisy. It didn't fool any one, though." She cackled and creaked with laughter as she shut the door.

Blanche sat motionless, staring straight before her, while the fire died out and the room grew cold.

Her terror and shame gave way at last, and she allowed herself to dream of the mystical joy of maternity. She permitted herself to fancy the life of a mother in a sheltered and prosperous home. She felt in imagination the touch of little lips, the thrust of little hands, the cling of

THE MOCCASIN RANCH

little arms. "My baby should come into a lovely, sun-lit room. It should have a warm, pretty cradle. It should—"

The door opened and her husband entered.

"Why, Blanche—what's the matter? You've let the fire go out. It's cold as blixen in here. You'll take cold, first you know."

VI

DECEMBER

WINTER came late, but with a fury which appalled the strong hearts of the settlers. Most of them were from the wooded lands of the East, and the sweep of the wind across this level sod had a terror which made them quake and cower. The month of December was incredibly severe.

Day after day the thermometer fell so far below zero that no living thing moved on the wide, white waste. The snows seemed never at rest. One storm followed another, till the drifting, icy sands

THE MOCCASIN RANCH

were worn as fine as flour. The house was like a cave. Its windows, thick with frost, let in only a pallid light at midday. There was little for Blanche to do, and there was nothing for her to say to Willard, who came and went aimlessly between the barn and house. His poor old team could no longer face the cold wind without danger of freezing, and so he walked to the store for the mail and the groceries. They lived on boiled potatoes and bacon, suffering like prisoners— jailed innocently. He hovered about the stove, feeding it twisted bundles of hay till he grew yellow with the tanning effect of the smoke, while Blanche cowered in her chair, petulant and ungenerous.

The winter deepened. There were many days when the sun shone, but the snow slid across the plain with a menacing, hissing sound, and the sky was milky with flying frost, and the horizon looked cold and wild; but these were merely the pauses between storms. The utter dryness of the flakes and the never-resting progress of the winds kept the drifts shifting, shifting.

"This is what you've dragged me into!" Blanche burst out, one desolate day after a week's confinement to the house. "This is your fine home — this dug-out! This is the climate you bragged about. I can't stay here any longer. Oh, my God, if I was only back home again!" She rose, and walked back and forth, her shawl trailing after her. "If I'd had any word to say about it, we never'd 'a' been out in this God-forsaken country."

He bowed his head to her passion and sat in silence, while she raged on.

"Do you know we haven't got ten

pounds of flour in the house? And another blizzard likely? And no butter, either? What y' goin' to do? Let me starve?"

"I *did* intend to go over to Bussy's and get back the flour they borrowed of us, but I'm a little afraid to go out to-day; it looks like another norther. The wind's rising, and old Tom—"

"But that's just the reason why you've got to go. We can't run such risks. We've got to eat or die—you ought to know that."

Burke rose, and began putting on his wraps. "I'll go over and see what I can squeeze out of old lady Bussy."

"Oh, this wind will drive me crazy!" she cried out. "Oh, I wish somebody would come!" She dropped upon the bed, sobbing with a hysterical catching of the breath. The wind was piping a high-keyed, mourning note on the chimney-top, a sound that rang echoing down through every hidden recess of her brain, shaking her, weakening her, till at last she turned upon her husband with wild eyes.

"Take me with you! I can't stay here any longer—I shall go crazy!" She turned her head to listen. "Isn't some one coming? Look out and see! I hear bells!"

Burke tried to soothe her in his timid, clumsy fashion.

"There, there, now—sit down. You ain't well, Blanche. I'll ask Mrs. Bussy to come—"

She suddenly seemed to remember something. "Don't talk to her. Go to Craig's. Don't go to Bussy's—please don't! I hate her. I won't be in her debt."

THE MOCCASIN RANCH

This pleading tone puzzled him, but he promised; and, hitching up his thin, old horses, drove around to the door of the shanty. Blanche came out, dressed to go with him, but when she felt the edge of the wind she shrank. Her lips turned blue and she cowered back against the side of the cabin, holding her shawl like a shield before her bosom. "I can't do it! It's too cold! I'd freeze to death. You'll have to go alone."

Burke was relieved. "Yes, you'd better stay," he said, and drove off.

Blanche crept back into the shanty and bent above the stove, shivering violently. She drew a long breath now and then like a grieving child. Life was over for her. She had reached the point where nothing mattered. She sat there until the sound of bells aroused her. "It's Jim!" she called, and rose to her feet, her face radiant with relief. Rivers came rushing up to the door in a two-horse sleigh and leaped out with a shout of greeting, though he could not see her at the frosted window.

A moment later he burst in, vigorous, smiling, defiant of the cold.

"Hello! All alone? How are you?"

A quick warmth ran through her chilled limbs, and she lifted her hands to him.

"Oh, Jim, I'm so glad you came!"

"Keep away—I'm all snow," he warningly called, as he threw off his cap and buffalo coat. "Now come to me," he said, and took her in his arms. "How are you, sweetheart? I can't kiss you—my mustache is all ice. Where's Burke?"

"Gone to Craig's."

He winked jovially while pulling the icicles from his long mustache.

"I thought I saw him driving across the ridge. I was on my way to the store, but when I saw his old rack-a-bone team I turned off to see you. How are you?" he asked, tenderly, and his voice swept away all her reserve.

"Oh, Jim, I'm not well. You must take me away, *right off*. I can't stay here another day—*not a day*."

He looked at her keenly.

"Why? What's the matter?"

She evaded his eyes.

"It's so lonesome here—" Then she dropped all evasion: "You know why—Jim, take me away. I can't live without you *now*. I'm going to be sick."

He understood her very well. His eyes fell and his face knotted in sudden gravity. "I was afraid of that—that's why I came. Yes, you must get out of here at once."

THE MOCCASIN RANCH

She understood him. "Oh, Jim, you won't leave me now, will you?"

"No. I didn't say anything about leaving you." He put his arm around her. "I'm not that kind of a man. You and I were built for each other—I felt that on that first ride. I guess it's up to me to take you out of this." He broke off his emotional utterance and grew keen and alert.

"I've been planning to go, and I'm almost ready—in fact, I could leave now without much loss, but I didn't come prepared for anything so sudden. My office furniture don't amount to much, and this team is Bailey's"—he mused a moment. "*Come!*" he said, with sudden resolution, "it's go now—we'll never have a better chance."

She turned white with dread — now that she neared the actual deed.

"Oh, Jim! I *wish* there was some other way."

He was a little rough. Her feminine hesitation he could not sympathize with.

"Well, there isn't. We've got to get right out of this. Hurry on your things. The wind is rising, and we must make Wheatland by five o'clock. I came out to hold down my claim, but it ain't worth it. I reckon I've squeezed all the juice out of this lemon. This climate is a little boisterous for me."

He brought in a blanket and warmed it at the fire while she wrapped herself in cloak and shawl.

"I'd better write a little note to—him."

"What for? I've got nothing against him, except that he saw you first. But I guess he's out of the running now. It's you and me from this day on."

THE MOCCASIN RANCH

"I hate to go without saying good-bye," she said, tremulously. "He's always been good to me," she added, smitten with sudden realization of her husband's kindness.

He perceived that she was in earnest. "All right—only it does no good, and delays us. Every minute is valuable now. The outlook is owly."

The plain was getting gray as they came out of the door, and the woman shrank and shivered with an instant chill, but Rivers tenderly tucked the robe about her and leaped into the sleigh.

"Now boys, git!" he shouted to the humped and wind-ruffled team, and they sprang away into the currents of powdered snow, which were running along the ground in streams as smooth as oil and almost as silent.

The sleigh rose and fell over the ridges

like a ship. Off in the west the sun was shining through a peculiar smoky cloud, gray-white, vapory, with glittering edges where it lay against the cold, yellow sky. Every sign was ominous, and the long drive seemed a desperate venture to the woman, but she trusted her lover as a child depends upon a father. She nestled close down under his left arm, clothed in its shaggy buffalo-skin coat, a splendid elation in her heart. She was at last with the strong man to whom she belonged.

This elation did not last long. Her sense of safety died slowly out, just as the blood chilled in her veins. She was not properly clothed, and her feet soon ached with cold, and she drew her breath through her teeth to prevent the utterance of moans of pain. She was never free now from the feeling of guardianship which is the delight and the haunting uneasiness of motherhood. "I must be warm," she thought, "for *its* sake."

She heard his voice above.

"I never'll settle in a prairie country again—not but what I've done well enough as a land-agent, but there's no big thing here for anybody—nothing for the land-agent now."

"Oh, Jim, I'm so cold! I'm afraid I can't stand it!" she broke out, desperately.

"There, there!" he said, as if she were a child. "Cuddle down on my knees. Be brave. You'll get warmer soon as we turn south."

Nevertheless, he was alarmed as he looked about him. He gathered her close in his arm, holding the robe about her, and urged on his brave team. They were hardly five miles from the shanty, and yet the storm was becoming frightful, even to his resolute and experienced brain. The circle of his vision had narrowed till it was impossible at times to see fifty rods away. The push of the wind grew each moment mightier. A multitudinous, soft, rushing, whispering roar was rising round them, mixed with a hissing, rustling sound like the passing of invisible, winged hosts. He could feel his woman shake with cold, but she spoke no further word of complaint.

He turned the horses suddenly to the left, speaking through his teeth.

"We must make the store," he said. "We must have more wraps. We'll stop at the Ranch and get warm, and then go on. The wind may lull—anyway, it will be at our backs."

As the team turned to the south the air seemed a little less savage, but Blanche still writhed with pain. Her hands suffered most; her feet had grown numb.

"We'll be there in a few minutes," Rivers cheerily repeated, but he began to understand her desperate condition.

A quarter of an hour later his team drew up before the door of the ranch-house. It seemed deliciously warm in the lee of the long walls.

"Well, here we are. Now we'll go in and get warm."

"What if Mr. Bailey is there?" she stammered, with stiff lips.

"No matter, you must not freeze."

He shouted, "Hello, Bailey!" There was no reply, and he leaped out. "Come, you must go in." He took her in his arms and carried her into the room, dim, yet gloriously warm by contrast with the outside air. "Feels good here, doesn't it? Now, while I roll up some blankets,

THE MOCCASIN RANCH

you warm— We must be quick. I'll find you some overshoes."

Blanche staggered on her numb feet, which felt like clods. She was weak with cold, and everything grew dark before her.

"Oh, Jim, I can't go on. I'll freeze. I'll die—I know I shall. My feet are frozen solid."

He dragged a chair to the hearth of the stove, in which a coal fire lay. His action was bold and confident.

"No, you won't. I'll have you all right in a jiffy. Trouble is, you're not half dressed. You need woollen underclothing and a new fur cloak. We'll make it sealskin to pay for this."

He unlaced her shoes and slipped them off, and, while she sobbed with agony, he rolled her stockings down and took her cold, white feet in his warm, swift hands.

In a few minutes the wrinkles of pain on her face smoothed out, and a flush came into her cheeks. The tears stood on her eyelashes. She was like a sorrowing child who forgets its grief in a quick return of happiness.

Suddenly Rivers stopped and listened. His face grew set and dark with apprehension. "Here, put your veil back, quick! It's Bailey! Don't answer him, unless I tell you to."

Outside a clear voice pierced through the wind. It was Bailey speaking to the horses.

Rivers went on, angrily: "If you'd been half dressed, this wouldn't have happened. There'll be hell to pay unless I can convince him—"

A hand was laid on the knob and Bailey entered.

"Hello, Jim! I didn't think you'd

THE MOCCASIN RANCH

come out to-day." He eyed the muffled woman sharply. "Who've you got with you—Mrs. Burke?"

"It don't concern you," Rivers replied. He saw his mistake instantly, and changed his tone. "Yes, I'm taking her home. Come, Mrs. Burke, we must be going."

"Wait a minute, Jim," said Bailey. He studied them both carefully. "Something's wrong here. I feel that. Where are you going, Jim?"

Rivers' wrath flamed out. "None o' your business. Come, Blanche." He turned to her. His tones betrayed him again.

Bailey faced him, with his back to the door.

"Wait a minute, Jim."

"Get out o' my way."

There was a silence, and in that silence the two men faced each other as if

THE MOCCASIN RANCH

under some strange light. They seemed alien to each other, yet familiar, too. Bailey spoke first:

"Jim, I know all about it. You're stealing another man's wife—and, by God, I won't let you do it!" His voice shook so that he hardly uttered his sentence intelligibly. The sweat of shame broke out on his face, but he did not falter. "I've seen this coming on all summer. I ought to have interfered before—"

Rivers laid a hand on him. "Stand out o' my way, or I'll kill you."

The quiver went out of Bailey's voice. He took his partner's hand down from his shoulder, and when he dropped it there was a bracelet of whitened flesh where his fingers had circled it. "You'll stay right here, Jim, till I say 'go.'"

Rivers reached for a weapon. "Will I?" he asked. "I wonder if I will?"

Blanche burst out: "Oh, Jim, don't! Please don't!"

The men did not hear her. They saw no one, heard no one. They were facing each other in utter disregard of time or place.

Bailey's tone grew sad and tender, but he did not move: "All right, Jim. If you want to go to hell as the murderer of your best friend, as well as for stealing another man's wife, do it. But you sha'n't go out of this door with that woman *while I live*. Now, that's final." His voice was low, and his words came slowly, but not from weakness.

For a moment hell looked from the other man's eyes. He was like a tiger intercepted in his leap upon his prey. The laugh had vanished from his hazel eyes — they were gray and cold and savage, but there was something equally forceful in Bailey's gaze.

Rivers could not shoot. He was infuriate, but he was not insane. He turned away, cursing his luck. His face, twitching and white, was terrible to look upon, but the crisis was over.

Bailey's eyes lightened. "Come, old man, you can't afford to do this. Go out and put up the team, and to-morrow we'll take Mrs. Burke home—I'll explain that she came over after the mail and couldn't get back."

Rivers turned on him again with a sneer. "You cussed fool, can't you see that she *can't* go back to Burke? I've made her mine—you understand?"

Bailey's hands fell slack. He suddenly remembered something. He brushed his hand over his brow as if to clear his vision:

"Jim, Jim, I—good God!—how could you do such a thing?" He was helpless as a boy, in face of this hideous complication.

Rivers pushed his advantage. He developed a species of swagger:

"Never mind about that. It's done. Now what are you going to do? Can you fix up such a thing as that?" Bailey was still silent. "It simply means that I'm her husband from this time on. Sit down, Blanche — I'm going to put up the team, but to-morrow morning we go. We couldn't make it now, anyway," he added. "There's nothing for it but to stay here all night."

Bailey stood aside to let him go out, then went to the stove and mechanically stirred it up and put some water heating. This finished, he sat down and leaned his head in his hands in confused thought.

To his clear sense his partner's act seemed monstrous. He had been brought up to respect the marriage bond, and to protect and honor women. The illicit was impossible to his candid soul. All the men he had associated with had been respecters of marriage, though some of them were obscene—thoughtlessly, he always believed—and now Jim, his chum, had come between a man and his wife! With Estelle in his mind as the type of purity, he could not understand how a wife could be the faithless creature Blanche Burke seemed. Her weakness opened a new world to him. He could not trust himself to speak to her.

The bubbling of the kettle aroused him, and he rose and went about getting supper. After a few moments he felt able to ask, with formal politeness:

"Won't you lay off your things, Mrs. Burke?"

She made no reply, but sat like an old

gypsy, crouched low, with brooding face. She, too, was wordless. She had made the curious mistake of looking to Bailey for justification. She had felt that he would understand and pity her, and his accusing eyes hurt her sorely. "If I could only speak? If I could only find words to tell him my thought, he would at least not despise me," she thought. Her face turned toward him piteously, but she dared not lift her eyes to his. He typified the world to her, and, furthermore, he was kindly and just; and yet he was about to condemn her because she could not make him understand.

Trained to laugh when she should weep, how could she plead overmastering desire, the pressure of loneliness and poverty, and, last of all, the power of a man who stood, in her fancy, among the most brilliant of her world. She felt herself in the grasp of forces as vast, as impersonal, and as illimitable as the wind and the sky, but, reduced to words, her poor plea for mercy would have been, "I could not help it."

Her maternity, which should have been her glory and her pride, was at this hour an insupportable shame. She had experienced her moments of emotional exaltation wherein she was lifted above self-abasement, but now she crouched in the lowest depths of self-suspicion. The rising storm seemed the approach of the remorseless judgment-day, the howl of the wind, the voice of devils, exulting in her fall.

She did not trouble herself about her husband. At times she flamed out in anger against his weakness, his business failures, his boyish gullibility. Sometimes she pitied him, sometimes she hated him.

THE MOCCASIN RANCH

She watched Bailey furtively. The firm lines of his face, his sturdy figure, and his frank, brusque manner were as familiar to her as the face of Rivers, and almost as dear—but she could not speak!

At last she gave up all thought of speaking, and drew her shawl about her with an air of final reserve. She resembled an old crone as she crouched there.

Rivers returned soon and took off his overcoat without looking at Bailey, who bustled about getting the supper, his resolute cheerfulness once more aglow.

Rivers sat down beside Blanche. "It would be death to attempt Wheatland to-night," he said. "I could make it all right, but it would be the end of you."

Bailey could not hear the words she spoke in reply. "Supper's ready," said he. "We all have to eat, no matter what comes."

THE MOCCASIN RANCH

Something in his voice and manner affected Blanche deeply. She buried her face in her hands and wept while Rivers sat helplessly looking at her. She could not rise and walk before him yet. The shame of her sin weighed her down.

Bailey poured some tea and gave it to Rivers.

"Take this to her while I toast her some bread."

She drank the tea but refused food, and Rivers sat down again still wearing an air of defiance, though Bailey did not appear to notice it. He ate a hearty supper, making a commonplace remark now and again.

Once he said, "We're in for a hard winter."

"It's hell on the squatters," Rivers replied, for want of other words. "I don't know what they'll do. No money and

THE MOCCASIN RANCH

no work for most of them. They'll have to burn hay. If it hadn't been for the price on buffalo bones, I guess some of them would starve."

Rising from the table, Bailey moved about doing up the work. He was very thoughtful, and the constraint increased in tension.

The storm steadily increased. Its lashings of sleet grew each hour more furious. The cabin did not reel, for it sat close in a socket of sods—it endured in the rush of snow like a rock set in the swash of savage seas. The icy dust came in around the stovepipe and fell in a fine shower down upon Bailey's hands, fell with a faintly stinging touch, and the circle of warmth about the fire grew less wide each hour. "If the horses don't all freeze we'll be in luck," said he.

The stove roared as a chained leopard

might do in answer to a lion outside. Slender mice came from their dark corners and skittered across the floor before the silent men, their sleek sides palpitating with timorous excitement.

Bailey hovered over the stove, trying to figure up some accounts. Rivers sat beside Blanche. With watchful care he kept her shawl upon her shoulders and her feet wrapped in a blanket. He spoke to her now and then in a voice inaudible to Bailey, who studied them with an occasional keen glance.

"Well, now," he said, at last, "no use sitting here like images; we might as well turn in. Jim, you take the bunk over there; and, Mrs. Burke, you occupy the bed. I'll make up a shake-down here by the stove and keep the fire going."

Rivers sullenly acquiesced, and Blanche lay down without removing her outside

THE MOCCASIN RANCH

garments, in the same bed in which she had slept that first night in this wild land —that beautiful, buoyant spring night. How far away it all was now!

Rivers heaped blankets upon her and tenderly tucked her in, whispered goodnight, and without a word to Bailey rolled himself in a fur robe and stretched himself on his creaking, narrow couch.

So, in the darkness, while the storm intensified with shrieking, wild voices, with whistling roar and fluttering tumult, Bailey gave his whole thought to the elemental war within. His mind went out first to Burke, who seemed some way to be the wronged man and chief sufferer, cut off from help, alone in the cold and snow. By contrast, Rivers seemed lustful and savage and treacherous.

Such a drama had never before come into Bailey's life. He had read of somewhat similar cases in the papers, and had passed harsh judgment on the man and woman. He had called the woman wanton and the man a villain, but here the verdict was less easy to render. He liked Mrs. Burke, and he loved his friend. He had looked into their faces many times during the last six months without detecting any signs of degradation; on the contrary, Blanche had apparently grown in womanly qualities; and as for Jim, he had never been more manly, more generous and kind. If their acts were crimes, why could they remain so clear of eye?

Without reaching a conclusion, he put the question from him and willed himself to sleep.

When he awoke it was morning, but there was no change in the wind, except in an increase of its ferocity. The roar was still steady, high-keyed, relentless.

THE MOCCASIN RANCH

A myriad new voices seemed to have joined the screaming tumult. The cold was still intense.

He looked at his watch and found it marking the hour of sunrise, but there was no light. The world was only a gray waste. He renewed the fire, and began preparations for breakfast, his sturdy heart undismayed by the demons without. Rivers, awakened by the clatter of dishes, rose and scraped a peep-hole in a window-pane. Nothing could be seen but a chaos of snow.

"No moving out of here to-day," he muttered, with a sullen curse.

Bailey assumed a cheerful tone.

"No; we're in for another day of it."

Inwardly he was appalled at the thought of what the long hours might bring to him. To spend twenty-four hours more in this terrible constraint would be ghastly. He set about the attempt to break it up. He whistled and sang at his work, calling out to his partner as if there were no evil passions between them.

"This is the fourth blizzard this month. Good thing they didn't come last winter. This land wouldn't have been settled at all. What do you suppose these poor squatters will do?"

Rivers did not respond.

Blanche tried to rise, but turned white and dizzy, and fell back upon the bed, seized with a sudden weakness. Rivers brought her some tea and sat by her side, while Bailey again toasted some bread for her. She looked very weak and ill.

Bailey went out to feed the horses, glad of the chance to escape his problem for a moment. Finding Rivers still sullen

THE MOCCASIN RANCH

upon his return, he got out some old magazines and read them aloud. Rivers swore under his breath, but Blanche listened to the reading with relief. The stories dealt mostly with young people who wished to marry, but were prevented by somebody who wished them to "wed according to their station." They were innocent creatures who had not known any other attachment, and their bliss was always complete and unalloyed at the end.

Bailey read the tender passages in the same prosaic tone with which he described the shipwreck, and his elocution would have been funny to any other group of persons; as it was, neither of his hearers smiled.

Blanche's heart was filled with rebellion. Why could she not have known Jim in the days when she, too, was young

THE MOCCASIN RANCH

and innocent like the heroines of these stories?

At noon, when Rivers went out to feed the team, Bailey went over toward the wretched woman. His face was kind but firm:

"Mrs. Burke, I hope you've decided not to do this thing."

She looked at him with shrinking eyes.

"What do you mean?"

"I mean you can't afford to go away with Jim this way."

"What else can I do? I can't live without him, and I can't go back."

"Well, then, go away alone. Go back to your folks."

"Oh, I can't do that! Can't you see," she said, finding words with effort—"can't you see, I *must* go? Jim is my real husband. I must be true to him now. My folks can't help me—nobody can help me but Jim— If he stands by me, I can live." She stopped, feeling sure she had explained nothing. It was so hard to find words.

"There must be some way out of it," he replied, and his hesitation helped her. She saw that he was thinking upon the problem, and found it not at all a clear case against her.

After Rivers came back they resumed their seats about the fire, talking about the storm—at least, Bailey talked, and Rivers had the grace to listen. He really seemed less sullen and more thoughtful.

Outside the warring winds howled on. The eye could not penetrate the veils of snow which streamed through the air on level lines. The powdered ice rose from the ground in waves which buffeted one another and fell in spray, only to rise again in ceaseless, tumultuous action.

THE MOCCASIN RANCH

There was no sky and no earth. Everything slid, sifted, drifted, or madly swirled.

The three prisoners fell at last into silence. They sat in the dim, yellow-gray dusk and stared gloomily at the stove, growing each moment more repellent to one another. They met one another's eyes at intervals with surprise and horror. The world without seemed utterly lost. Wailing voices sobbed in the pipe and at the windows. Sudden agonized shrieks came out of the blur of sound. The hours drew out to enormous length, though the day was short. The windows were furred deep with frost. At four o'clock it was dark, and, as he placed the lamp on the table, Bailey said,

"Well, Jim, we're in for another night of it."

THE MOCCASIN RANCH

Rivers leaped up as if he had been struck.

"Yes, curse it. It looks as if it would never let up again." He raged up and down the room with the spirit of blasphemy burning in his eyes. "I wish I'd never seen the accursed country."

"Will you go feed the team, or shall I?" Bailey quietly interrupted.

"I'll go." And he went out into the storm with savage resolution, while Bailey prepared supper.

"The storm is sure to end to-night," he said, as they were preparing for sleep. As before, Blanche lay down upon the bed, Rivers took the bunk, and Bailey camped upon the floor, content to see his partner well bestowed.

Blanche, unable to sleep, lay for a long time listening to the storm, thinking disconnectedly on the past and the morrow. The strain upon her was twisting her toward insanity. The never-resting wind appalled her. It was like the iron resolution of the two men. She saw no end to this elemental strife. It was the cyclone of July frozen into snow, only more relentless, more persistent—a tornado of frost. It filled her with such awe as she had never felt before. It seemed as if she *must not sleep*—that she must keep awake for the sake of the little heart of which she had been made the guardian.

As she lay thus a sudden mysterious exaltation came upon her, and she grew warm and happy. She cared no longer for any man's opinion of her. She was a mother, and God said to her, "Be peaceful and hopeful." Light fell around her, and the pleasant odors of flowers. She looked through sunny vistas of oaks and apple-trees. Bees hummed in the clover, and she began to sing with them, and her low, humming song melted into the roar of the storm. She saw birds flying like butterflies over fields of daisies, and her song grew louder. It became sweet and maternal—full of lullaby cadences. As she lay thus, lovely and careless and sinless as a prattling babe, her eyes fixed upon the gleam of lights in the dark, a shaking hand was laid on her shoulder, and Rivers spoke in anxious voice:

"What is it, Blanche?—are you sick?"

She looked at him drowsily, and at last slowly said: "No, Jim—I am happy. See my baby there, in the sunshine! Isn't she lovely?"

The man grew rigid with fear, and the hair of his head moved. He thought her delirious—dying, perhaps, of cold. He gathered her hands in his and fell upon his knees.

"What is it, dear? What do you mean?"

"Nothing, nothing," she murmured.

"You're sure you're not worse? Can't I help you?"

She did not reply, and he knelt there holding her hands until she sank into unmistakably quiet sleep.

He feared the unspeakable. He imagined her taken in premature childbirth, brought on by exposure and excitement, and, for the first time, he took upon himself the burden of his guilt. The thought of danger to her had not hitherto troubled him. For the poor, weak fool of a husband he cared nothing; but this woman was his, and the child to come was his. Birth—of which many men make a jest—suddenly took on majesty and terror,

THE MOCCASIN RANCH

and the little life seemed about to enter a world of storm which filled him with a sense of duty new to him.

He bent down and laid his cheek against his woman's hands, and his throat choked with a passionate resolution. He put his merry, careless young manhood behind him at that moment and assumed the responsibilities of a husband.

"May God strike me dead if I don't make you happy!" he whispered.

VII

CONCLUSION

BAILEY woke in the night, chilled. The fire was low, and as he rose to add some coal to the stove he looked about him in his way. Rivers' bunk was empty. He glanced toward the bed, and saw him wrapped in his buffalo coat kneeling beside Blanche's pillow. He seemed asleep, as his cheek rested upon his right hand, which was clasped in both of hers.

The young pioneer sat for several minutes thinking, staring straight at his friend. There was something here that made all the difference in the world. Suppose these people really loved each other as he loved Estelle? Then he softly fed the fire and lay down again.

His brain whirled as if some sharp blow had dazzled him. Outside the implacable winds still rushed and warred, and beat and clamored, shrieking, wailing, like voices from hell. The snow dashed like surf against the walls. It seemed to cut off the little cabin from the rest of the world and to dwarf all human action like the sea. It made social conventions of no value, and narrowed the question of morality to the relationship of these three human souls.

Lying there in the dark, with the elemental war of wind and snow filling the illimitable arch of sky, he came to feel, in a dim, wordless way, that this tragedy was born of conventions largely. Also, it appeared infinitesimal, like the activities of insects battling, breeding, dying. He came also to feel that the force which moved these animalculæ was akin to the ungovernable sweep of the wind and snow—all inexplicable, elemental, unmoral.

His thought came always back to the man kneeling there, and the clasp of the woman's hands—that baffled him, subdued him.

When he awoke it was light. The roar of the wind continued, but faint, far away, like the humming of a wire with the cold. He lay bewildered, half dreaming, not knowing what it was that had impressed him with this unwonted feeling of doubt and weariness. At last he heard a movement in the room and rose on his elbow. Rivers was awake and was peering out at the window.

THE MOCCASIN RANCH

Blanche replied to his words of greeting with a low murmur—"I feel very weak."

She seemed calmer, also, and her eyes had lost something of their tension of appeal.

Bailey looked at her closely, and his heart softened with pity. He waited upon her and tried by his cheerful smiles to comfort her, nevertheless.

They ate breakfast in silence, as if apprehending the struggle which was still to come.

At last Rivers rose with abrupt resolution.

"Well, now, I'll bring the team around, and we'll get away."

"Wait a minute, Jim," Bailey said. "I want to say something to you." There was a note of pleading in his voice. "Wait a little. I've been thinking this thing over. I don't want you to go away feeling hard toward me." His throat choked up and his eyes grew dim. "I don't want to be hard on you, Jim. It's a mighty big question, and I'm not one to be unjust, specially toward a woman. Of course, somebody's got to suffer, but it hadn't ought to be the woman—I've made up my mind on that. Seems like the woman always does get the worst of it, and I want you to think of her. What is to become of her?"

Blanche turned toward him with a wondrous look—a look which made him shiver with emotion. He looked down a moment, and his struggle to speak made him seem very boyish and gentle.

"I can't exactly justify this trade, Jim, but I guess it all depends on the *mother*. She ought to be happy anyway, whether you are or not; so if she thinks she'd

THE MOCCASIN RANCH

better go with you, why. I ain't got a word to say."

Blanche gave a low cry, a cry such as no woman had ever uttered in his presence, and fell upon her knees before him.

The cadence of her moan cut deep into his heart. He realized for the first time some part of her suffering, her temptations. Her eyes shone with a marvellous beauty. He was awed by the rapt expression of her face.

"Don't do that," he stammered. "Please get up."

"You're so good!" she breathed.

"Oh no, I'm not. I don't know—I don't pretend to judge—that's all. Yesterday I did, but now—well, I leave the whole business with you and God. Please stand up."

She rose, but stood looking upon him with a fixed, devouring look. He had never seen tears in her eyes before. She had been gay and sullen and tense and sad, but now she was transfigured with some emotion he could not follow. Her eyes were soft and dark, and her pale face, sad and sweet, was instinct with the tenderness of her coming maternity. The sturdy plainsman thrilled with unutterable pity as he looked down upon her.

There was a silence, and then Rivers came to Bailey's side, and said, brokenly,

"Rob, old man, you've done me good —you always *have* done me good—I'll be faithful to her, so help me God!"

Bailey understood him, and shook his hand. They stood for a moment, palm to palm, as if this were in some sense a marriage ceremony. Bailey broke the tension by saying:

"Well, now get your team—I wouldn't

THE MOCCASIN RANCH

let you take her out into the cold only I know she ought to be where a doctor can be reached. The quicker you go the better."

While Rivers was gone he turned to her and helped her with her cloak and shawl. His heart went out toward her with a brother's love. He talked with cheerful irrelevancy and bustled about, heating a bowlder for her feet and warming her overshoes.

"Now it's all right. Jim will take care of you. Don't worry about Will; I'll go over and see him." He wrapped her in every available blanket and shawl, and at last helped her outside and into the sleigh. He tucked the robe around her while Rivers held the restless horses. His voice trembled as he said:

"Now, Jim, get her under shelter as quick as you can. Leave the team at

Wheatland. I'll come after it in a day or two. I want to see somebody in town, anyway."

The woman turned toward him. He saw her eyes shine through her veil. She bared her hand and extended it toward him. "I hope you and Estelle will be happy."

He covered her hand with both of his. The gesture was swift and tender. It seemed to shield and forgive. Then drawing the robe over it without a word, he briskly said, "Well, Jim, I guess this is the fork in the road," and he looked at his chum with misty eyes. Rivers turned away, and they again clasped hands without looking at each other.

"Good-bye, old man," said Rivers.

"Good-bye, Jim, and *good luck!*"

Bailey saw his partner draw the woman close down under the shelter of his shoulder, while his powerful hand whirled the team to the south.

He stood in the lee of the shanty until the swift sleigh was a slowly moving speck on the plain, then he went in and sat down to muse on the wondrous last look in the woman's eyes. "I wonder what Estelle will say?" he asked himself, and a sense of loneliness, of longing to see her, filled his heart with dreams.

THE END

first edition